For Kay

WHAT WE DO
A HUTCHINSON BOOK 0 09 188496 9

Published in Great Britain by Hutchinson,
an imprint of Random House Children's Books

This edition published 2004

1 3 5 7 9 10 8 6 4 2

Text and illustrations copyright © Reg Cartwright, 2004

RANDOM HOUSE CHILDREN'S BOOKS
61–63 Uxbridge Road, London W5 5SA
A division of The Random House Group Ltd

RANDOM HOUSE AUSTRALIA (PTY) LTD
20 Alfred Street, Milsons Point, Sydney,
New South Wales 2061, Australia

RANDOM HOUSE NEW ZEALAND LTD
18 Poland Road, Glenfield, Auckland 10, New Zealand

RANDOM HOUSE (PTY) LTD
Endulini, 5A Jubilee Road, Parktown 2193, South Africa

THE RANDOM HOUSE GROUP Limited Reg. No. 954009
www.kidsatrandomhouse.co.uk

A CIP catalogue record for this book is available from the British Library.

Printed in Singapore

What We Do

Reg Cartwright

HUTCHINSON
LONDON SYDNEY AUCKLAND JOHANNESBURG

We are worms and we wiggle.

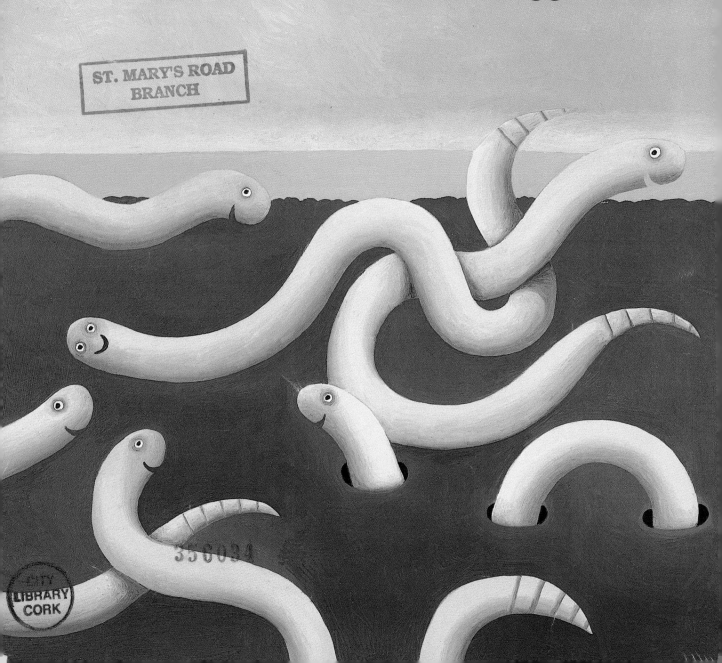

I'm a caterpillar, I creep.

I'm a fish and I swim.

We are lambs and we leap.

I'm a monkey and I swing.

We are penguins and we waddle.

I'm a kangaroo, I jump.

We are geese and we paddle.

I'm a moth and I flutter.

I'm a mouse and I scurry.

We are ants and we march.

We are always in a hurry.

I'm a frog and I hop.

I'm a dog and I dig.

I'm a bird and I fly.

And I guzzle – I'm a pig!

I'm a squirrel and I climb.

I'm a snake and I slide.

I'm a hippo and I wallow.

I'm a swan and I glide.

I'm a crab and I crawl.

I'm a donkey and I bray.

I'm a giraffe and I stretch.

We are children and we play.